Other books by Mick Inkpen:

KIPPER

KIPPER'S TOYBOX

ONE BEAR AT BEDTIME

THE BLUE BALLOON

THREADBEAR

BILLY'S BEETLE

PENGUIN SMALL

British Library Cataloguing in Publication Data

A catalogue record for this book is
available from the British Library

ISBN 0 340 57952 8

Text and illustrations copyright © Mick Inkpen 1993

The right of Mick Inkpen to be identified as the author
of this work has been asserted by him in accordance with
the Copyright, Designs and Patents Act 1988.

First published 1993

Published by Hodder and Stoughton Children's Books,
a division of Hodder and Stoughton Ltd,
Mill Road, Dunton Green, Sevenoaks, Kent TN13 2YA

Printed in Italy by L.E.G.O., Vicenza

Kipper's Birthday

Mick Inkpen

HODDER & STOUGHTON

London Sydney Auckland

It was the day before Kipper's
birthday. He was busy with his
paints making party invitations.
In large letters he painted,

Plees come to my bithday party
tomoro at 12 o cloc dont be lat

He hung them up to dry and set
about making a cake.

Kipper had not made a cake before. He put some currants and eggs and currants and flour and sugar and currants into a bowl. Then he stirred the mixture until his arm ached.

Next he added some cherries and stirred it once more. Then he rolled it with a rolling pin and looked at what he had made.

'I have made a flat thing,' he said.

Kipper squeezed the flat thing into a cake shape and watched it bake in the oven. To his surprise it changed itself slowly into a sort of heap, but it smelled good. He put the last remaining cherry on the top for decoration.

By this time the party invitations were dry.

'I'll deliver them tomorrow,' yawned Kipper. 'It's too late now.'

Kipper woke bright and early on his birthday. His first thought was, 'Balloons! We must have balloons!' But as he rushed downstairs another thought popped into his head. 'Invitations!'

Kipper ran all the way to his best friend's house and stuffed the invitations into Tiger's hand.

'That one's yours! Those are for the others!' he panted. 'Can't stop! Balloons!'

When he had gone Tiger opened the invitation.

Plees come to my bithday party tomoro at 12 o cloc dont be lat

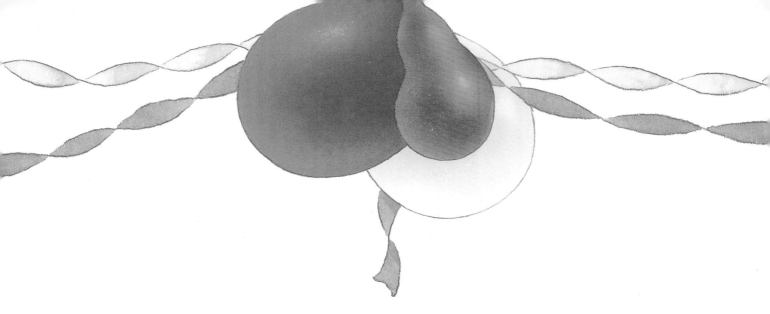

At twelve o'clock Kipper carefully placed his cake on the table and sat down to wait for a knock at the door.

He waited. And he waited. But nobody came. Not even Tiger.

The cake smelled good and Kipper began to feel hungry. At one o'clock he ate the cherry from the top.

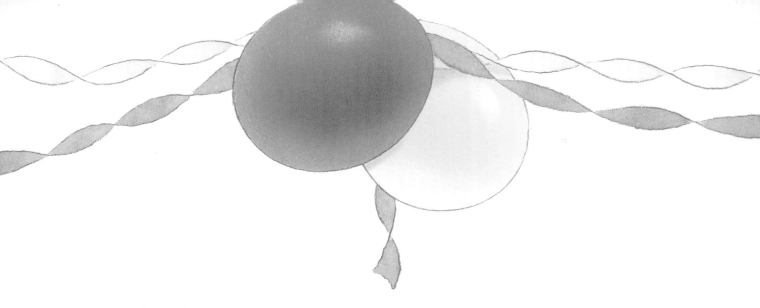

Two o'clock passed. Still nobody came. Kipper pulled off a large piece of cake and broke it open to see if there was a cherry inside. There were two. He ate them both and began to feel better.

By five o'clock there were no more cherries to be found.

Kipper stretched out on the table feeling very full and very sleepy.

Kipper slept through the
evening and into the night.
He dreamt that he was
climbing a mountain made of
cake and dodging great cake boulders
as they crashed towards him.

Even when the sun streamed
through his window the next morning
he did not wake, but snored
peacefully until noon
when he was woken by
a knock at the door.

His friends had come.
'Happy birthday,
Kipper!' said Jake.
'Happy birthday,
Kipper!' said Holly.
'And many happy
returns!' said Tiger.
Kipper blinked and
rubbed his eyes.
'But my birthday
was yesterday,' he
said sleepily.

They looked at the invitation.

Plees come to my bithday party tomoro at 12 o cloc dont be lat

Kipper looked puzzled.
'So my birthday is not until tomorrow,' he said. 'We haven't missed it after all!'

'No, no, no,' said Tiger. 'Your birthday must have been *tomorrow* the day before yesterday.' Kipper looked puzzled again.

Tiger went on, 'So yesterday it would have been *today,* but today it was *yesterday.* Do you see?'

Kipper did not see. His brain was beginning to ache so he said, 'Cake anyone?' And then he remembered that he had eaten it all.

'Never mind,' said Tiger. 'Why don't you open your presents?'

The presents seemed a bit odd.
The first was a napkin from Jake.
The second was some candles from Holly.

'Very useful,' said Kipper, trying not to look disappointed.

But the third was the most useful of all…

It was a cake!